THE
GHOSTS OF
HUNGRYHOUSE
LANE

THE GHOSTS OF HUNGRYHOUSE LANE

Sam McBratney

Inside illustrations by Lisa Thiesing

AN **APPLE** PAPERBACK

SCHOLASTIC INC.
New York Toronto London Auckland Sydney

ISBN 0-590-43462-4

Text copyright © 1988 by Sam McBratney. Inside illustrations copyright © 1989 by Lisa Thiesing. All rights reserved. Published by Scholastic Inc., 730 Broadway, New York, NY 10003, by arrangement with Henry Holt and Company, Inc. APPLE PAPERBACKS is a registered trademark of Scholastic Inc.

12 11 10 9 8 7 6 5 4 3 2 1   0 1 2 3 4 5/9

Printed in the U.S.A.   40

First Scholastic printing, May 1990

Contents

THE
GHOSTS OF
HUNGRYHOUSE
LANE

1...

The House
in Hungryhouse Lane

When Mercia Porterhouse died at the age of eighty-six, she left her house and its ghosts to her best friend, Miss Amy Steadings. Amy ran a shop in the village of Tunwold near Hungryhouse Lane.

Amy didn't get the house, though. Nobody could find Mercia's will.

"But I *know* that she made a will," Amy said firmly to the lawyer—a smart young lady in a gray suit. "I was right there when she signed it, and Thomas Addiddle signed it too. He was the butcher until the wind blew him off the roof of his barn, poor soul. And there was a very special reason why dear Mercia wanted me to have her house, and nobody else."

She meant the ghosts, of course, but didn't like to say so in just so many words in case the young lady in the gray suit misunderstood. People sometimes re-acted very strangely to the word "ghost."

"Miss Steadings," said the lawyer with just a hint of impatience, "I can only tell you that this will did not turn up among the personal effects of the deceased. Naturally I shall continue to make inquiries on your behalf . . ."

"And her diary is missing," continued Amy. "I know that Mercia had a diary—she wrote it up every night of her life. And what about her book?"

"Which book is that?"

"She was writing a book called *The Ghosts of Great Britain*, and where has *it* gone to, I'd like to know. They have boards all over the windows so that nobody can see in. That'll be her nephew's doing, I'll be bound. He lives in Venezuela, you know. Mercia didn't like him one bit!"

The lawyer, who had been pretending to take notes until this moment, set down her fountain pen and rose to her feet. "I think I have all the details I need for the moment, Miss Steadings. Leave this with me and I shall see what I can do."

Without that will there was nothing she could do. Some months went by, and the nephew of Mercia Porterhouse, acting through his London lawyers, put the house in Hungryhouse Lane up for rent.

The Sweet kids didn't know a thing about ghosts.
Can a ghost fly a helicopter? Can you take its photo?
2...

Would a ghost eat toast, does it sneeze when it gets pepper up its nose and does it even *have* a nose? These were questions that Zoe, Charlie and Bonnie Sweet had never asked themselves before they arrived in Hungryhouse Lane.

They came in the family's new Mercedes. Mr. Sweet was driving when the car lurched into Hungryhouse Lane. He believed that he drove much better than Mrs. Sweet, and this suited both of them very well, since she much preferred to sit and look around at the sights instead of the boring old road.

They were rich. Until two months ago Mr. Sweet had sold insurance policies for a living—then he won a fortune in the lottery and hadn't done a day's work since. This gave him lots of free time to play backgammon. Both Mr. Sweet and Mrs. Sweet were backgammon addicts; they played for hours on end and sometimes conducted rather savage postmortems on their games. Such a conversation was happening as the Mercedes drove up Hungryhouse Lane.

"You were lucky," said Mr. Sweet. "If you hadn't come up with a six and a one you would have been beaten hollow. Sheer luck."

"No, no," said Mrs. Sweet, smiling smugly, "I had the game sewn up on account of my superior play."

"Superior play? Such piffle! Superior play!" The car shot forward—as if it, too, were angry—and Zoe Sweet cried out from the backseat, "There it is! Slow down, Daddy, or you'll pass it."

...3

A stately pair of wrought-iron gates stood open as if someone had known that they were coming. Double rows of marvelous cedar trees darkened the avenue as the car crunched up the drive.

"Great trees!" said Mr. Sweet. "They must be a hundred years old!"

"We should give the trees a birthday party, shouldn't we, Daddy?" said little Bonnie sweetly, holding up her doll so it could see out the window. Its name was Lulubelle. The bashed-up, bald-headed thing had just survived its second birthday party, having been punched, bitten, kicked and even buried alive (by Charlie Sweet) in its short life. It looked much, much older than the trees.

"Does this dump have a pond?" asked Charlie.

"We don't know if it has a pond, dear," said his mother.

"How can my tadpoles grow up to be frogs if there's no pond?" The tadpoles in question sat on Charlie's knee in a coffee jar. A state-of-the-art camera dangled from a strap around his neck. Charlie was very keen on tadpoles and photography.

"You were told not to bring them but you brought them," said his sister Bonnie. "Serve you right if they shrivel up and die, murderer."

"Thumbsucker," said Charlie quietly.

At the mere mention of this powerful word, Bonnie's doll Lulubelle lost her sense of reason and belted Charlie on the cheek, which made him lash out with

4...

his feet. His feet hit the dog. Muldoon howled, and some lively drops of water escaped from the coffee jar.

"Mommy, he's spilling water over me," shrilled Zoe. "*Frog* water, Mommeeeeee!"

For the third time on that particular journey the Mercedes shrieked to a halt, dangerously close to one of the grand old cedars.

"Children," said Mr. Sweet through clenched teeth, "I cannot drive with that racket going on. CUT IT OUT! How would you like us all to be killed?"

No answer was possible to such a stupid question. It produced a silence that lasted until they emerged from the shade and set eyes on their new home.

It was one of those houses that seem to consist, curiously, more of roof than of walls. The beautifully manicured thatch rippled over two small attic windows that reflected rectangles of passing clouds, like a pair of watchful eyes. Indeed, the whole house, situated as it was within a round of mature, native trees, appeared to have an air of great patience. The twisted stems of ivy running up the walls had already invaded the thatch with thin, clutching tendrils and may have given the house a rather sinister kind of charm—but Charlie didn't think so.

"It looks like a big haystack with specs on," he said poetically, then took a photo.

"But did you ever see such an ugly chimney!" cried Mrs. Sweet, referring to a yellow-brick monstrosity tacked on to a gable's end.

"Oh!" declared Bonnie, clapping her hands with excitement. "I do hope we get good TV reception!"

Standing in the shadow of a huge elm tree, Mr. Sweet now fished from his pocket a stubby brass key. It seemed such a tiddly little thing to open such a massive door.

"I bet it creaks," said Zoe, but in fact the door opened noiselessly. The first member of the Sweet family to enter was Muldoon, who sneaked through all their legs and hopped up onto a white-sheeted chair.

Mr. Sweet went off to find the fuse box, Mrs. Sweet unpacked the backgammon board, Bonnie hunted through a footlocker for some videos and Charlie upended his jar of lukewarm frog spawn into the kitchen sink. Out they came with many a gurgle, slop and plop.

"That is absolutely revoltingly disgusting!" shrieked Zoe. "That is our kitchen sink, it is not for yucky taddies, it is *communal*."

"Spell that," said Charlie.

"C-O-M-M-U-N-A-L."

"Wrong," said Charlie. "I said spell *that*. T-H-A-T."

"Oh, funny funny. That joke is as old as the hills."

"It still got you, sucker."

"Mommy!" Zoe Sweet ran through the house, still raving. "He is putting his stinking frog spawn into the kitchen sink and it is COMMUNAL."

The Sweet family had arrived in Hungryhouse Lane.

2...

The Sweet Kids

It was a jolly good thing for someone that there was only one house in Hungryhouse Lane, and that Tunwold Village lay two miles up the road and comfortably out of range of the Sweets. They were a rather noisy family.

Zoe was the eldest child and inclined to be rather excitable. As the lawyer of the family she tended to be bitterly disappointed when her brother and sister failed to do exactly what she ordered them to. "Mommy, it isn't right!" she would cry, or, "Daddy, it just isn't fair!" There are lots of people just like Zoe in the world, who insist that other people should always obey all the rules. As well as being very bossy, she was a very courageous girl and had a good brain. She expected to get top grades in all her classes.

Charlie, the middle Sweet, could be quiet, brooding and cunning: Perhaps this was because his sisters ganged up on him rather a lot. Until Muldoon joined the family, his best friend was an invisible pet rhinoceros that no one believed in but Charlie—not even when its mighty footprints were discovered on the front lawn early one morning. Of course Charlie had matured since those days, especially since he'd taken up photography. He photographed everything, great and small, from his granny's spare set of false teeth to Lulubelle drowning face downward in a rain barrel. The local pharmacist said that he was an excellent photographer for a boy of only nine.

As for little Bonnie Sweet, people generally regarded her as a darling child until they witnessed one of her temper tantrums. These began with a crumpled face and ended with her lying on her back and kicking the wall as high as she could reach with her heels. She really could scream until she turned dangerously blue. For a child so young, Bonnie had an extraordinary degree of control over her feelings: She could love you, hate you, charm you, ignore you and reduce you to pitying her, just by pressing the appropriate emotional buttons. A great career awaited her on the stage.

Muldoon Moonbug Nelson Sweet was the sixth member of the family. (Each of the children had given the poor dog a name.) It was a mongrel with foxy ears and a long, dachshund-type body, like one of those things people put along the bottom of a door to keep out the draft. Muldoon's tail was a mere stump, and he closed his eyes when he barked. On no account would he agree to sleep out-of-doors, and he refused all brands of canned dog food. Clearly he regarded himself as one of the Sweet kids.

They were interesting children but not particularly nice. They squabbled and fought rather like starlings around a single crust of bread. There is no doubt that their behavior might have worried some parents, but Mr. and Mrs. Sweet scarcely gave them a second thought. They were much too busy playing backgammon and reading the *Financial Times*.

That evening—their first in Hungryhouse Lane—a row broke out in the upper part of the house. Little Bonnie took one look at her bedroom and began a shriek of protest.

"Mommy, this is not my room. I want one of those rooms with the straw around the windows!"

"It's called thatch, dear."

"I don't care what it's called, I *want* one, and so does Lulubelle."

"Bonnie, this *is* one of those rooms. Look out of the window and you will see the thatch."

"Oh." The temper-tantrum tap was turned off when Bonnie looked out and saw the thatch. She also noticed an elderly lady riding an old black bike along the lane.

Then Bonnie went next door to have a look at her

sister's bedroom and discovered that Zoe had one of those delightful old four-poster beds with lovely swishy curtains all around it.

"I want one too," said Bonnie.

"There is only one," said Mrs. Sweet, so Bonnie cast herself to the floor, rose up on her shoulder blades and assaulted the wall mercilessly with her feet.

"Geoffrey!" called Mrs. Sweet. "Will you come and deal with this, please."

Mr. Sweet arrived, took his screaming daughter by the ankles, carried her away upside down and set her in an ancient cast-iron bath. Muldoon, sickened by the din, trotted up a small flight of stairs to find Charlie.

In some ways Charlie Sweet was quite disappointed by his room. He certainly disliked the huge, high bed—the idea of falling out of that thing in the middle of the night didn't appeal to him one bit, and besides, Charlie often allowed his feet to hang out of the bed at night so that Muldoon could lick them. On the other hand the room had lots of nooks and corners that made it interesting.

One of the first things he did was to take his camera to the window and peer through the zoom lens at the distant roofs of Tunwold Village. First a parade of slow-moving, boring old cows crossed his viewfinder. Then he spotted a small wood. How nice it would be, thought Charlie, if there happened to be a local wolf living over there. Suddenly a movement caught his eye, but sadly it was not a wild beast—it was an old lady riding her bike along Hungryhouse Lane. Charlie took her picture and then started to unpack.

He had uncovered his favorite sneakers and dartboard when he noticed something odd in the corner of the room. It was, he thought at first, a curious trick of the light—a shapeless blur reflecting off a shiny surface. Whatever it was, though, appeared to want to organize itself into a definite shape, and after five or six seconds Charlie imagined that he could make out the ghostly folds of a full dress.

It was a woman—wasn't it? She'd come from nowhere! Unfortunately the blob at the top that might have been a large hat was centered on his dartboard and seemed unclear. He didn't dare blink in case the image disappeared, but a scuffling noise behind made him turn around (Muldoon had just bolted under the bed), and when Charlie looked again, the shape was gone.

Blast it! thought Charlie. I should have taken a picture. Then a voice called out from far below.

"Charlie Sweet, come down here this minute and get these tadpoles out of the kitchen sink!"

Down in the kitchen, pots and pans had been produced. Zoe busily opened a can of beans and Bonnie cheerfully filled the drawer with cutlery as if she had never been stuck away in a cast-iron bath. Mr. Sweet was trying very hard to connect a brand-new dishwasher to aging copper pipes, and just above his head

Mrs. Sweet beat up some eggs in a bowl. It was all very homely.

"Do you want baked beans or an omelette, Charlie?"

"Omelette. I saw a spook in a hat," said Charlie.

"Oh, sure," said Zoe, who remembered her brother's invisible rhinoceros. "I bet it was wearing pink pajamas and rubber boots, as well."

"What did it say?" Bonnie seemed genuinely curious.

"It didn't say anything. It just stood there for a minute and looked me in the eye; then it sort of shook a fist at me and the room went freezing cold. Muldoon saw it too, didn't you, Muldoon?"

Muldoon looked up, lay down and wagged his stump of a tail to show his pleasure at getting a mention, but Mrs. Sweet was not pleased.

"Geoffrey, that child is telling those stories again. Speak to him, please."

Geoffrey, just then, had skinned his knuckles on the concrete floor and now leveled a trembling monkey wrench at his son. "Listen, my boy, it took us two years to get rid of your blasted invisible rhino that messed up our front lawn, and if I hear any more nonsense about spooks, you'll go to your bed at eight o'clock!"

It was ten past eight already, but Charlie got the message. He scooped up the slimy slurps of frog jelly in his fingers and returned them to their original jar.

"Okay. It was just my imagination," he said.

14...

3...

Lady Cordelia and Sir James

What Charlie had just seen upstairs was not due to his imagination at all, for he had just seen the ghost of Lady Cordelia McIntyre. And what a fright he had given her, too!

Who was he, she wondered, that funny-looking little boy with that thing around his neck; what on earth was he doing in the bedroom of Mercia Porterhouse; and where was dear Mercia, anyhow? Lady Cordelia rapidly withdrew through the bedroom wall and elevated her Presence through the ceiling and into the attic.

Had she been seen by him? It was possible that she had, in spite of her evasive action. She was *very* annoyed with herself, for any ghost worthy of the name can easily avoid being seen unless it is absolutely pitch dark.

Cordelia hovered in the attic twilight, her soft and elegant outline turning like a ballerina on a music box. Her husband had been with Lord Clive in old India. One day, as she was bathing a scab behind her elephant's ear, the grateful beast had patted her gently with its trunk and finished her off on the spot.

They shot the offending elephant, which Cordelia did not like one bit, but of course she was only a ghost by that time and couldn't do a thing about it. They turned Rajah's tusks into chess pieces and his feet into umbrella stands. Ghosts, people sometimes fail to realize, tend to haunt *things* rather than *places*—they usually attach themselves to something connected with what made them ghosts in the first place, and Cordelia, for her part, took refuge in one of Rajah's feet. And this foot, now an umbrella stand, somehow came into the possession of Mercia Porterhouse.

Like most ghosts Cordelia was a quiet soul whose only ambition was to enjoy long periods of Unwakeful Serenity*—she had no time at all for that clanking of chains and wailing in the night that a small minority of ghosts seemed to go in for, and indeed she had not "materialized" since 1979.

Now, in Mercia's attic, she fingered nervously the phantom jewelry at her neck. So poor Mercia, born when the twentieth century was but seven minutes old,

*This is a ghostly condition. You may like to think of Unwakeful Serenity as a kind of hibernation.

had finally Traveled On. What was to happen now? she wondered. Should she waken James, who lived in a carboy—a large glass bottle—in the attic, and tell him?

Better not, she decided. James was such a twittery fellow, there was no telling what he might do. "Oh dear," Cordelia thought aloud, "I do so hate uncertainty." So she condensed her vapory form into dear old Rajah's foot and decided to forget. After all, sometimes the nasty things of life simply went away.

The very next day, however, Cordelia became unpleasantly aware of the sound of raised voices close by. The tramping of careless feet caused the attic floor and Rajah's foot to tremble as they had never trembled before, and a dog, of all things, barked practically in her ear.

"Die!" someone cried. "Die, die, die, you dirty devil!" Cordelia swirled upward in alarm, carefully situating her Presence in the pool of light pouring through the skylight. A girl came prancing through the attic, wielding a bamboo walking stick as if it were a two-edged sword. "Gotcha!" she screamed.

Gracious! Such unseemly language. This was unnecessarily violent behavior from a girl. And that boy, the one she had seen yesterday, was making horrible faces at himself in a full-length mirror. The youngest of the children seemed a sweet little thing in a flowery dress—until she picked up Rajah's foot and tossed it to one side, saying, "What a grody piece of moldy old junk."

Lady Cordelia McIntyre was obliged to watch as the three horrors ransacked the attic from one gable's end to the other. Occasionally something made them pause—an item of clothing from a trunk, a doll's house, a box of lead soldiers—but nothing made them wonder for long. They sampled the contents of every drawer and every box large and small, without the slightest show of respect or discipline, whooping all the while like the robbers of some old tomb.

Then that boy whipped up a handmade rug in a cloud of dust and said, "Oh boy! Look what I've got here."

He lifted up a large, green bottle.

"It's the biggest bottle I've ever seen," said the younger girl. "Can I have it please, Charlie?"

"No."

"What's inside it?" asked the other girl.

"Nothing. But there soon will be—this is exactly what I've been looking for!" And off the boy went, cradling the bottle in his arms and looking as though he might drop it at any moment.

By now Cordelia was all of a quiver. They were taking James away with them! He had been a Presence inside that carboy for the best part of two hundred years, and now he was being carted downstairs by a young ruffian in a vulgar red cardigan!

Of course she had to follow and see what happened. By drifting vertically downward Cordelia actually arrived before them in the kitchen, where she became an undetectable Presence in the misty light streaming through a window. The two adults scarcely looked up from their game of backgammon when the children burst in.

"Mommy, look what we found in the attic. It's the biggest bottle ever seen and can I have it, please?"

"Certainly, Bonnie dear."

"She's not getting it. I found it and it's mine!" shouted Charlie.

"Mommy, it's not his and he's going to put his taddies in it, and it's too beautiful for stinking frog spawn."

Oh dear, thought Cordelia. Frog spawn! James would hate that; ghosts could not tolerate damp.

"Geoffrey—sort this out."

The father laid down his dice, sighed and scowled.

"Children, how can we possibly play backgammon with this constant bickering going on? Who found the bottle?"

"Charlie did."

"Then Charlie can have it."

The girl started up a howl and ran out the back door. She kept on running and she kept on howling. The dreadful sound faded away in the far distance.

A jar appeared from under the sink. The boy fished

out globules of transparent jelly and fed them sloppily through the neck of the carboy, and really, thought Cordelia, it was a revolting sight. She could easily see why the Creator should make a great and noble creature like the elephant, but why on earth did He bother with slimy, hopping things like frogs? Poor James. Carefully allowing herself to rise, Cordelia returned to the attic through two ceilings.

And there was James, shimmering with indignation among the thatch pegs. His enormous wig trembled uneasily on his head as if it might topple over. It had been very fashionable, at the time when James had become an ex-human being, for gentlemen to wear a lacy handkerchief at the wrist so that they could dust the snuff from the back of the hand. That hanky, now, seemed to be doing a furious dance of its own as James let fly with his arms.

"Cordelia, I have the most awful thing to tell you. You cannot guess what has just happened to me, it is . . . indescribable!"

"They threw frog spawn all over you, James."

"You were there? You saw? Oh, the indignity of it is appalling!"

Sir James Walsingham had been one of London society's most eligible bachelors. One evening, while he was attending one of Lady Gilzean's glittering functions, a mouse jumped out of his wig and caused his hostess to swoon at the dinner table. Unfortunately someone referred to James as a bounder for harboring a rodent like that. Insults were swapped, faces were slapped and a duel was arranged without further ado. James was no swordsman, so he chose pistols and was shot through the heart the following dawn. In this way he became an ex-human being. How he ended up in a glass bottle is another story.

Two hundred years later he was all of a twitter as he surveyed the attic in Hungryhouse Lane.

"Who are those horrible children? And look at this place that was our home—what has become of it?" The lace hanky began to flutter in panic. "And my carboy! Where shall I spend my periods of Unwakeful Serenity, for heaven's sake?"

"Calm down, James, please."

"I don't want to calm down. I feel doomed—what is an egg without its shell, answer me that. Oh, for a moment of Genuine Presence, I would go down there and punch them on their noses!"

"Don't be silly, James," said Cordelia, who had expected all of this, and more. "The last time you punched a nose you got yourself shot. We have to think about these events intelligently."

James did not enjoy criticism. He became silent and glum—but only momentarily. "And where is Mercia? How can she allow such savages to run amok like this, I'd like to know."

"I'm afraid, James, that poor Mercia's race is run."

"What race?"

"She's dead, James."

"Lucky for some. And anyway, that doesn't explain anything—where is Amy Steadings? Mercia always said she would leave her house to that shopkeeper after she was gone. Don't tell me *she's* gone and died on us too!"

"I don't know. Perhaps we might visit Amy some evening when there is no wind and see what has happened. Meanwhile I suggest that we simply make do."

Craftily James eyed Cordelia's elephant's foot.

"Look here, Cordelia, now that I've lost my carboy, I'm in a bit of a pickle. You wouldn't care to share your elephant's foot with me, by any chance?"

Cordelia was shocked by the very idea and quickly let him know it. "Most certainly I would *not*, James. What would Colonel McIntyre think of such a thing?"

Colonel McIntyre had been dead and gone since 1798 and had Rested in Peace ever since. All the same, breeding was breeding and one could not simply ignore it because one happened to be a ghost. James spent that night around a dry and dusty old chandelier.

4...

The West Chimney

Now and then the Sweet children cooperated with one another.

This didn't happen often, mind you—they seemed to get more thrills out of bickering loudly over inconsequential things—and when it *did* happen, the reason had to be pretty important. As, for example, when all three of them ran out of pocket money at the same time.

Their plan was hatched in Zoe Sweet's clever brain. They chose a time when Mommy and Daddy Sweet were engrossed in a backgammon thriller. Bonnie wormed her way onto her daddy's lap with Lulubelle in her arms and whispered, "Daddy, could you give me fifty pence please so I can buy some sweets for Lulubelle?"

"Too many sweets aren't good for Lulubelle's teeth, dear," replied her father.

Bonnie kissed her daddy's cheek. "Don't be a silly, Daddy. Lulubelle's only a dolly!"

She got her money. Then Zoe appeared a little later.

"Mom, I'm going into the village. Could you let me have some pocket money, please?"

"You've had your pocket money for this month, Zoe dear. You must learn to manage."

"But Bonnie got fifty pence from Daddy. It's not fair if she gets money and I don't."

"Fetch me my purse, then."

"And what about me?" asked Charlie, who popped up as if by magic when he heard the click of his mother's purse opening.

Suitably armed with small change, they set off for Tunwold Village. It hardly needs to be said that the Sweet children did not walk pleasantly along the country roads playing I Spy With My Little Eye and other games in tune with the quiet surroundings. Instead they beheaded primroses, threw stones at rooks' nests, had a nettle fight through the bars of the farmer's gate and hurled insults at a scarecrow in a field.

"Hey, turnip head!"

"Hick face!"

"Yo! Zoe wants you for a boyfriend!"

Muldoon, meanwhile, ventured into a field on the other side of the road to attack a herd of grass-munching black-and-white beasts. One of these beasts stopped munching to stare at the noisy intruders, then lurched forward with two large and menacing steps—whereupon Muldoon turned his other end to the cow and ran for his life.

"You coward, Muldoon!" jeered the Sweet kids.

Tunwold Village consisted of one long street and two cobbled cul-de-sacs. It boasted three antique shops, a shop that sold paintings, another that sold horsy things, a jeweler's and very little else.

"What a dump," said Bonnie, speaking for all of them. "It doesn't even have a supermarket."

"Look over there, though," Zoe said, pointing. "That shop on the dark side of the street sells candy."

Above the shop it said PERCIVAL STEADINGS—TOBAC-CONIST TO GENTLEMEN. The word *confectioner* appeared in small print, as if by afterthought. The shop window didn't look all that promising—it was full of pipes and big stone jars with labels on them like YELLOW OLD GOLD and DR. JOHNSTON'S SPECIAL MIX. A bell clanged once when Charlie opened the door.

"Yuck! The place stinks," said Zoe, holding her nose. "Grab your doses, everybody."

They held their noses—except for Muldoon, of course—until a voice startled them. "What you smell is tobacco."

Amy Steadings wore her hair in a tight bun at the

back of her head. Her wine-colored blouse was fastened at the neck by a brooch that seemed to catch the light from the window and send it out in sparks. Her eyes sparkled too, but even so Zoe reckoned that she was probably ancient.

"That's what I sell," said Amy Steadings. "Tobacco. But you nice children surely don't want to buy tobacco."

"We certainly don't," said Zoe. "Smoking is a filthy habit and it's bad for you and it stinks up everybody's air."

"I'll have a packet of bacon-flavored crackers, please," said Bonnie, holding up her money.

"Bacon flavor? Goodness me, whatever next. I can give you a packet of plain, dear, or cheese and onion, but folk around here don't ask for bacon."

"Cheese and onion, then."

"And I'll have a bag of M&Ms, please," said Charlie.

A jar appeared on the counter. Amy Steadings continued to talk as she unscrewed the lid with great care, rather like a bomb-squad officer dealing with a suspect device. "I wonder, would you be the new children who live in Hungryhouse Lane? I thought so, yes. I knew the lady who lived there before you. A lovely lady, so kind. I supplied her with oriental tobaccos for many years."

"She smoked a *pipe*?" shrieked Zoe.

"Oh yes—one bowl in the evenings, rather like Sher-

lock Holmes. Now then, dear, would you like barley sugar or peanut brittle? Folk around here don't ask much for M&Ms."

"If you ask me, folk around here don't ask much for anything," grumbled Zoe.

"I'll have peanut brittle," said Charlie.

The hard candy fell like stones into a little brass pan, and from the brass pan into a tiny white bag.

"I was wondering, children, have you come across any of my friend's . . ." Amy Steadings hesitated, as if the proper word eluded her. ". . . Any of her . . . pets?"

"She hasn't got any pets," said Charlie. "If she has, they're all dead."

The shopkeeper smiled oddly. "Listen. If I give you some barley sugar from my other jar, will you do something a little bit special for me?"

"Yes," said Zoe at once.

"I will," said Bonnie.

"Me too," said Charlie.

"It's a small thing, really, but quite important. I would like you to tell your mommy and daddy not to light a fire in the west chimney."

The Sweet children glanced at one another. This was a very funny way to earn a few free pieces of candy.

"You mean the big yellow one?"

"Yes."

"Why not?" asked Charlie.

"Because my friend had that chimney specially built. You see, it was dismantled in Manchester, brick by brick, and brought all the way to Hungryhouse Lane."

"But we'll be cold without a fire," said Bonnie.

"Child, dear," said Amy Steadings, "that house has central heating in every room."

"But what's wrong with it? Is it broken? Does it smoke?" Zoe persisted.

"Well, no, not exactly," said Amy, setting out three barley sugars for each of them, excluding Muldoon. "You will do that for me, won't you?" And she set out a fourth barley sugar each, to be sure.

As the Sweet children wandered out of Tunwold Village, they ate crackers, sucked barley sugars and shared mouthfuls of pink lemonade from a quart bottle. When at last they got around to conversation, they discussed how to compel Mommy and Daddy to buy them a horse. Or even three horses. Then Zoe changed the subject.

"What did that woman mean by pets? And why would her friend who owned our house build a chimney out of bricks from Manchester and never even light a fire in it?"

"She was probably batty," said Charlie. "You can easily go that way, living in the country."

"Imagine, she smoked a pipe!" said Bonnie. "Whoever heard of a woman who smoked a pipe?"

"Concentrate, you two!" Zoe said sharply. "It couldn't

be that the chimney is a fire hazard—I heard Daddy say that the thatch has been treated with fire-resistant stuff, so . . . Charlie! What do you think you are doing?"

Charlie was busily pulling rotten sticks from the hedgerows.

"I'm going to light a fire."

"Where?"

"In the big chimney. If there's something funny about it, let's find out what it is."

This was such an interesting idea that Bonnie and Zoe began to gather up sticks by the armful too. When the Sweet kids arrived back at the house in Hungry-house Lane, even poor old Muldoon had so many sticks shoved under his collar that he resembled a hedgehog.

5...

James Decides to Act

Sir James Walsingham was driving Lady Cordelia McIntyre nuts with his antics. He floated upside down among the roof beams, waving his hanky and sighing great, sad sighs as if his world had come to an end.

"Oh for goodness' sake, will you stop it, James!" Cordelia told him firmly. "And please will you stay the proper way up. It is *very* disconcerting to have to look at your head down there."

"It's all very well for you," James retorted tartly. "They didn't put frog spawn in your elephant's foot."

Eventually he came to rest in an upright position against the wall of the west chimney, where he plucked nervously at the outline of his wig, just as he used to do in real life. "And may I point out," he added sourly, "that those horrors have left the skylight open."

This was a reference to the fact that ghosts do not like rapidly moving air. They tend to be easily blown about, rather like the seed heads of dandelions.

Cordelia, listening intently to something else, told him to be quiet. "Shh. I hear something. What is that roaring noise?"

James listened too. "It's one of those hateful modern things that look like wasps."

He meant a helicopter. Cordelia shook her head and gasped. Slow, curling, thin coils of smoke seeped through the attic wall and passed right through James's head as if they were coming from under his wig.

"Smoke!" she cried. "Oh no! James, they've gone and lit a fire in the west chimney! *Surely* not."

"Of course they have," said James dramatically, for the smoke had now engulfed him. "The vile beasts are capable of anything. I could have told you that something like this would happen. Look, there's our sooty friend from Manchester."

A thin, wispy wraith of a ghost had materialized through the wall of the west chimney and now looked about her with wide, cautious eyes. Over her shoulder she carried a set of chimney brushes.

This was Bobbie, the third of Mercia Porterhouse's ghosts and the old lady's favorite. It was impossible to tell that Bobbie was a girl just by looking at her, for her foster parents had cut off most of her hair (more than a hundred and fifty years ago, now) so that she

could get up chimneys and earn money like the other climbing boys; and she was dressed, besides, in a pair of coarse and baggy trousers. These were so badly torn at the knees that James could hardly bear to look at them.

James had very little to do with Bobbie. He liked people to be attired in something approaching good style, and the little sweep, frankly, was an eyesore. Anyway, she never spoke a word—not a word!—and James thrived on clever conversation and gossip. Naturally he was sorry that she'd had such a hard life, but as a child of the serving classes, well, it was to be expected.

But Cordelia said, "Bobbie, you poor, dear thing," and tried to put a motherly arm around her shoulder. "Oh, if Mercia could see you now, she would be *so* angry, and after all the trouble she took to provide you with Unwakeful Serenity. I'm afraid we have some shocking news for you, Bobbie."

"You can say that again," said James, sniffing a pinch of imaginary snuff. "The house has been taken over by a bunch of frog lovers. You *do* know what a frog is, I take it?"

Bobbie stared at him blankly.

"*Frogs*. They are slimy and green and they hop. Good grief, they must have had frogs, even in Manchester."

Bobbie shook her head.

"Don't be silly, girl, of course they had frogs; there

are frogs everywhere. You were too busy climbing chimneys to notice, that's all."

Bobbie made a rather rude gesture with her brushes.

"I saw that!" cried James. "I saw it!"

"Oh, do stop it, James," Cordelia intervened. "You know how it upset dear Mercia to hear you shout at Bobbie, and I won't have it. The question we have to ask ourselves is, What are we going to do now?"

The time had come for some serious thinking. Already James had lost his carboy—who could guess what other drastic changes might lie in store for them? How could they get back to doing what a ghost does best and simply let the years roll by in a state of Unwakeful Serenity?

"I have a plan," said James, "if you would like to hear it."

"Of course we would. If it's a sensible plan, James."

"Scare them off. Let us appear before the little horrors in the middle of the night when everything is quiet and still and very, very dark. Make them shake in their shoes! Let them know the house is well and truly haunted! That should shake up the rotters!" He drew his phantom sword and struck a fine pose. "As ex-human beings, we *are* ghosts, after all."

"I don't know. Perhaps we ought not to be too aggressive to begin with. Wouldn't it be nice to discover that they are perfectly reasonable people and to come to an arrangement with them, rather like the one we had with Mercia? Probably they're not yet aware that we exist together under the same roof, and rowdy children often have hearts of gold. What do you think, Bobbie?"

Bobbie pointed her brushes at Cordelia to show that she preferred this second plan.

"Good. Then it's settled. I shall speak to them tomorrow in a friendly way and try to make them understand our situation. If worse comes to worst, we can always try a little haunting later."

Through the rest of that evening and for the early part of the night James was in a foul mood. The sheer boredom of being a conscious ghost was something he found utterly intolerable. As he drifted about the attic, listing to one side and then to the other, he cursed that silly little mouse that had been his downfall all those years ago. How had the little blighter got into his wig, anyhow? Foul play, probably. Good grief, it wasn't as if his head was dirty. He washed it—and his wig!—at least five times a year! A mouse of all things. How are the mighty fallen!

Then he heard a door opening in the lower part of the house. Soundlessly he passed through the attic floor and saw the smallest of the horrors walking along the landing in her nightie and slippers. What was she doing out of bed fifteen minutes after midnight? James could not help thinking that here was the perfect opportunity to scare her out of her skin. He positively glowed with excitement as she came toward him.

How should he do it? He could ooze out of a wall

and whisper some little word like "Boo!" Or he could drift up the banister rail, reaching out to her with both hands. Why not materialize out of a picture, sword in hand! Or he could rise out of the floor at her feet, rather like those ghosts used to do in the plays by that fellow Shakespeare. James, who had not had such fun in ages, was still making up his mind when the girl suddenly opened a door and went into a room.

She reappeared almost immediately. James was about to give her the fright of her life when he saw something that made him think again. She was carrying his beloved carboy!

Along the landing she staggered, the frog spawn swilling from side to side within the green glass. If she dropped it, by jove, he was in trouble. Broken carboys, James thought soberly, stay broken forever. So he waited and watched.

The girl emptied the frog spawn into a bowl, pressed a little handle, and the whole lot disappeared with a gurgle and a whoosh. And she hadn't finished yet. Down the stairs she went, carrying the carboy with her, through the back door into the night. It was far too windy for James to venture out, so he watched from a window and saw her hide the bottle in the heart of a large, leafy bush.

What a jolly interesting show, thought James. He was about to return to the attic and give an account of these events to the others when he paused and thought again. Why not go through with his original plan? Of course, Cordelia was right to say that they were only children—but they had no business being here upsetting everything and everybody with their tadpoles and their noisy nonsense. Besides, they had no manners to speak of, and people with no manners had no right to complain about anything. It was time they learned that they were not alone. . . .

James allowed himself to drift through the wall of Bonnie Sweet's room.

6...

Bonnie Sees a Ghost

Breathlessly Bonnie closed her bedroom door as quietly as could be and then tiptoed over to the window. She wanted to make double sure that she knew which bush the big bottle was under.

A little shiver ran up her arms where the breeze felt cool on her skin. Busy clouds scudded across the face of the moon as if they were going to a meeting on the other side of the sky. Bonnie kicked off her slippers and skipped into bed, feeling rather pleased with herself.

It wasn't right that such a lovely, big green bottle should be used for moldy old frog spawn—Bonnie was quite certain that the person who had made that bottle wouldn't like it a bit. Of course, Charlie would *guess*, but he wouldn't actually *know*, she'd put them down the toilet, and anyway he would soon forget about them, and one day Bonnie would "find" the bottle by accident and it would be hers. Besides, it would pay him back for burying Lulubelle in that horrible hole under the hedge.

Now she lay back, counting the beams in the roof and thinking very hard about horse names. Primrose, Flopsy or Fudge would be nice. Soon Daddy would buy her a proper riding outfit with a nice hard hat. She was thinking how Fudge was a really lovely name for a horse when she realized that her room, somehow, had become different.

She didn't know how, or why—it just was. Bonnie sat up in bed, suddenly seized by one of those feelings that come to you in the dead of night: Someone was watching her. Only when the wind drew a curtain of clouds across the moon did she see the tall, pale stranger standing in the half dark of the window bay.

Bonnie tried to let loose a big shout at him, but her voice came out as a funny little squeak. She armed herself with a pillow and threw Lulubelle at the intruder, but Lulubelle passed right through him and hit the far wall with a thump. Then she raced for the light switch and turned on the light with trembling hands and saw that he was still there, right in the middle of the room and drifting toward her—a great big spook with one hand on his sword and a high, impossible hairdo.

"Are you a ghost?" Bonnie shrilled. "Are you? Don't you come near me or I'll scream and I'll scream."

The ghost stretched out an arm, the one with the hanky on the sleeve, and performed an incredible bow. His dipping wig almost hit the floor.

"Enchanté, mademoiselle," it said.

That did it. Bonnie took off down the landing in a state of rare excitement, yelling hoarsely with the full force of her lungs. "Zoe, Zoe, where are you! Oh, Zoe!" She burst through the curtains of the four-poster bed. "You'll never believe it but it's real, you should see what I saw and Charlie was right—it's as really really real as could be!"

Zoe's eyes were open, but her mind was still a sleepy blank. "Bonnie, what is it?"

"In my room! It didn't walk but it had feet! Can you imagine, they just hung there like useless dangly-down bits. Oh, yes, it had a *sword*. It just sailed toward me, and Lulubelle went right through it. Oh, Zoe!"

A noise occurred at the door, which made Bonnie spin around in case the thing had followed her. But it was only Charlie arriving with Muldoon.

"What's up?"

"Charlie, you were right, it just came toward me, walking on air."

"Bonnie," said Zoe rather crossly, "are we supposed to read your mind?"

"It was a ghost." Bonnie's features were alive with the terrible excitement of it all. "It spoke to me in Russian or something. Isn't it *wonderful*?"

And a curious smile began to make its way across the face of Charlie Sweet. "So I wasn't seeing things. Oh boy, what a break. We've got our very own spook!"

7...

Lady Cordelia
Makes Herself Known

The Sweet children, including Muldoon, spent the rest of the night in Zoe's four-poster bed. They were full of hope that the ghost would appear again so that they could get a really good look at it. When it failed to do so, they all dropped off to sleep at more or less the same time—Charlie still with his camera around his neck.

In the morning, when Charlie discovered that his frog spawn were missing, war broke out again. Bonnie Sweet fled along the landing and down the stairs in her nightie at breakneck speed, pursued all the way by her brother, and had almost made it to the front door when she was brought to the floor by a flying tackle.

"Right! You ripped off my taddies!"

"I didn't, I didn't!"

"Yes, you did, you did, you *did*, you did!"

Mr. and Mrs. Sweet were reading the *Financial Times* when Bonnie burst in howling, to show off her brand-new black eye. Charlie was there too, roaring at the top of his voice.

"Children!" Mrs. Sweet clapped her hands once and put on her cross voice. "This will not do. Your father and I came to the country for peace and quiet; we did not come out to the country to be deafened by nonsense."

"But she stole my—"

"Be *quiet*. Geoffrey—speak to them."

Mr. Sweet folded his paper fiercely. "I can promise you that if this goes on we will send the three of you packing to boarding school."

"And there will be no horse," added Mrs. Sweet, with a very definite nod of her head.

These were powerful threats and they caused quite a silence. After some moments Bonnie spoke up softly.

"Mommy, if we get a horse, can its name be Fudge, please?"

"If you're a good girl—yes."

"Why should she get to name our horse?" Zoe inquired indignantly. "That's not fair, Mommy. I want to call it Jiffy."

"*I* shall name the horse," said Mrs. Sweet. "If there *is* a horse. Now do something useful, the three of you, and go out and tidy up that stable. It wouldn't be decent to put a *pig* into such a place, never mind a horse!"

This was not an exaggeration, as the children found when they arrived in the stable with brushes and pans

46...

to clean it out. Cans of old paint and rusted tools littered the shelves and the sills of the narrow windows. Clumps of old straw ("Left over from the ark," grumbled Charlie) turned to powder as soon as they were touched. Horsy relics of former days, now gloomy with neglect, hung from huge nails—and the paint, the tools, and the horsy relics and the disused drinking troughs and the broken timbers and the filthy windows were all linked to one another by an amazing, ongoing curtain of delicate cobwebs.

"How can there be so many yucky, awful spiders in the world?" wondered Zoe, who had donned roller skates. She zoomed across the concrete floor on wheels, pushing a mighty brush and raising a cloud of dust around her brother.

Charlie didn't notice. He was staring into the hayloft above. Up there, gliding among some tattered hay bales, was a gorgeous ghost.

"Oooooooo," said Bonnie. "It isn't the same one. This one's a *she!*"

The ghostly lady drifted down, down, down and landed close by with the perfect softness of a bubble. Her outline billowed slightly in the breeze from the stable door, and this same breeze played with the ringlets cascading down her bare shoulders. Muldoon, who did not like people he could see through, bolted.

"Oh dear," said the ghost, "I'm afraid I startled your dear little dog. Please don't be alarmed, I mean you no harm. Indeed . . ." the ghost smiled very graciously,

". . . I very much hope we can be friends. What are your names?"

"Zoe."

"Bonnie."

"I'm Charlie."

"How do you do? I am Lady Cordelia McIntyre. I think we've already met, Charlie, isn't that correct? I do so admire your shoes with wheels, Zoe. How absolutely fascinating!"

Zoe glanced down at her feet. "They're roller skates!"

"How many spooks are there in this place?" asked Charlie, who wondered whether he should make a bolt for his camera.

"There are three of us, actually." The ghost gave a little "ahem," as if polite chitchat was now over and this was business. "I've been meaning to speak to you for some time, as a matter of fact. You see, I live in the elephant's foot in the attic. Sir James Walsingham lives in the large glass bottle, although sadly he cannot live there now because you put frog spawn into it. Little Bobbie lives in the large west chimney, although she cannot live there anymore if you continue to light fires in it. And that is why I am speaking to you today. I should like to ask you, if I may, to leave us alone, please. It is such an awkward thing to be a ghost. One is so betwixt and between—can you understand that?"

"No," said Bonnie truthfully. "Why do you have clothes on? Do you get cold? Who does your hair like that? Can anybody be a ghost?"

The ghost smiled tolerantly and seemed to be about to answer at least one of these questions when Zoe butted in. "Suppose we don't agree to leave you alone? What then?"

"Well . . ." the ghost hesitated, as if to choose her words carefully. "I think you should remember that this house actually belongs to Miss Amy Steadings, who lives in Tunwold Village. Mercia Porterhouse left it to her in her will, and she didn't intend that you children should be here at all. In these circumstances surely you have an obligation to live and let live. If not, we *could* make life rather unpleasant for you."

"How?" asked Charlie. But the ghost persisted in being cheerful.

"Let's not talk about such things! I can see that you are good-hearted children, and that you will do your best to help us. Won't you? And now I must go."

"Do you eat spiders?" asked Bonnie.

"Gracious me, no." The ghost seemed appalled by the very idea. "It has been my pleasure to meet you, and I hope you will think over what I have said until we meet again. And now—good-bye." And up she rose, feather light, through the roof of the hayloft.

"Oh, I wish I could do that!" said Bonnie.

"Boy, she's some spook!" said Charlie.

"And she's never even seen roller skates," said Zoe Sweet. "How stupid can you get?"

8...

The Ghosts Change Their Plans

Cordelia reported back to James and Bobbie in an optimistic frame of mind.

"Well, I really do feel that they are not bad children. They listened very carefully to what I had to say. Without going into detail, I made a very strong appeal to their better natures, and I would say that in general they are sympathetic to us."

"Huh!" snorted James. He was thinking how that little beast had not been very sympathetic to her brother's frog spawn. "But what did they *say*?"

"Well, they asked a lot of questions. Naturally."

"Did they agree to share the house with us? Am I going to get my carboy back? I bet you didn't even ask."

"I mentioned your carboy, James, and that is quite

enough for the moment. I think we must bide our time and win their trust."

Balderdash! thought James, who sent himself drifting across the attic in a horizontal pose. From this angle he enjoyed a clear view, through a small roof window, of the old walled garden far below. This garden had once been the pride and joy of Mercia Porterhouse, but now it was a paradise for every weed under the sun. The three children were there, busily hammering nails into planks of wood.

"I don't trust them, not an inch," James muttered to himself. "What could the little schemers be making?"

In his opinion Cordelia was far too soft—what they needed was a few short, sharp shocks to their nerves— paralyze the beggars with fright! He realized, of course, that he'd been far too polite last night. He should have drawn his sword and threatened to cut off that little girl's head.

He allowed himself to sink through two floors into the great parlor, where two people sat over a backgammon board. James parked his Presence behind an aspidistra and listened.

"If you hadn't thrown double threes, I would have beaten you hollow."

"*If.* Let's have no sour grapes. You were outmaneuvered and out-thought."

"Out-thought! I like that! What about that time two

months ago when I beat you fourteen times in a row!"

It was an extraordinary scene. James thought that they must be playing for money, but there was no sign of it. He passed them by and made an exit through the French windows. It was a lovely, soft day outside. Within the walled garden there was scarcely a breath of wind, and the air was filled with bird song. James, approaching through a forest of lupines, observed that the children had stopped hammering in order to study their handiwork. They had made three signs out of planks and old boards. The first one said, in bold red paint:

STOP
VISIT THE GHOSTS OF HUNGRYHOUSE LANE.

James almost had a fit there and then among the lupines. The second sign said:

SEE THE SPOOKS IN OUR NOOKS.

And the third, most explicit of all, made the intentions of the little horrors absolutely plain:

BUS PARTIES WELCOME. ONLY TEN PENCE A PERSON.

"I wonder if ten pence is enough," said the larger female horror, the one with wheels on her feet. "I mean, it isn't every day you get to see a real ghost."

"Okay, I'll double it."

"Triple it."

... 53

The boy dipped a stick into a can of red paint and amended the figure accordingly.

"Those spooks are worth a fortune!" said the little female horror. "We're going to be millionaires, like Daddy."

James had heard quite enough. Making maximum speed for a ghost and muttering, "Mercenary little beasts!" he made a beeline for the attic with this latest piece of news.

Cordelia and Bobbie listened in shocked silence as James described the scene in the garden below with all its ghastly implications.

"So much for trust! So much for biding our time!" cried James. "The house is to become a *zoo*, and guess who are the main attractions. Us! We shall never have a moment's peace."

"Oh dear," said Cordelia limply. "I was obviously wrong about those children." She looked at Bobbie, and thought how miserable her poor, short life had been on earth and how she surely deserved better than this. "How cruel."

"I should think so," thundered James, now thoroughly aroused. The idea of people paying to get in to see him as if he were a peep show made him draw his sword and declaim in a grand manner: "Let us have done with kind words and fancy speeches. It is them or us! Let us strike a blow for Unwakeful Serenity. What we need is . . . action!"

Perhaps, thought Cordelia. But James, with his high wig, lacy hanky and transparent sword did not look terribly frightening.

Just at that moment Bobbie allowed herself to fade away through the wall of the west chimney. And presently, from the heart of the chimney, there began to spread through the house a long, undulating wail.

"WAAAAAAAAAA WAAAAAAAAAA!"

The sound was certainly not human, yet it could not have been mistaken for a natural occurrence—the wind growling in the chimney, for instance.

"By jove!" said James, who was most impressed.

"That is wonderful, Bobbie," Cordelia said when the little sweep reappeared. "I never knew you could make a noise like that. It is *perfect* for haunting, isn't it, James?"

Bobbie seemed pleased but didn't say a word.

"Promising," agreed James, returning his sword to its scabbard, "but let's wait until the sun goes down. We'll get them out of their beds in the middle of the night. *That's* the way to make them leave Hungryhouse Lane forever!"

9...

Attack!

Midnight had come and gone.

The Sweet kids spoke in whispers at the foot of Charlie's bed.

"Flashlight."

"Check."

"Paint."

"I got the paint," said Bonnie, shaking an aerosol spray. Zoe ticked the word *paint* on her list.

"Pepper."

"Check."

"Water bombs."

Charlie reached under the bed and produced a tray of fragile, bulging missiles. "Yep, we got water bombs."

"Rope."

"Why do we need a rope?" whispered Bonnie. "Even if we capture one, how can we tie it up?"

"Listen, moonbeam," explained her brother, "there are millions of things we don't know about ghosts. We're bringing this stuff just in case."

"Camera."

"Check."

The camera was very important. The Sweet kids, having decided that there was money in spooks, needed three or four pictures for their advertising campaign. They tiptoed up the dark flight of stairs to the attic in the following order: Zoe with the flashlight and the aerosol spray; Charlie with the rope around his shoulder and the camera around his neck; Bonnie with the tray of water bombs and the pepper shaker; and finally Muldoon, who did not look happy. In fact, when the spookhunting party halted outside the small half door into the attic, he let out a yelp that sounded distinctly nervous.

"Shh!" scolded Bonnie. "You'll wake up Mommy and Daddy."

"It wouldn't matter much," said Zoe. "They'd probably start playing backgammon. I'll go in first, okay? You two follow me in and Charlie gets the light switch. Ready—"

Ready, steady go, she was about to say—but that was the very moment when the noise began.

"WAAAAAAAAAAA WAAAAAAAAAAA!"

"It's that noise again!" hissed Bonnie, trying not to shout. "Which one of them is it, do you think?"

"Time to find out!" cried Zoe, kicking open the door and throwing herself inside the attic, where the beam of her flashlight cut crazy patterns in the darkness.

The stillness of the attic was shattered within seconds. The stamping of feet and the wailing of the ghosts and the shrieks of the Sweets were loud enough—but louder by far was the howling of that mad dog Muldoon.

"Gimme some light!" yelled Charlie, who couldn't remember where the switch was, and Bonnie began to dance and to scream, "There's one over here! Shine, shine!"

The ghost called James, suddenly trapped in a beam of light, waved his hanky in dismay.

"He's drawing his sword. Let him have it!"

Bonnie let fly with some pepper, Zoe let fly with some paint. Charlie, meanwhile, had found the light switch. "Look, there's the one from the elephant's leg!"

Lady Cordelia stood next to a long mirror, and every wisp of her insubstantial form spoke eloquent testimony to her feelings of shock, outrage and disapproval at this invasion of her privacy.

"Get her picture, Charlie, she's melting away!"

There came a dazzling flash from the camera. Muldoon, with both eyes shut, was barking hysterically at a third shape that had just come through the attic wall.

"Ooooo! It's the chimney spook!" cried Bonnie.

"I bet she's the noisy one," yelled Zoe. "Let her have it!"

A terrible assault now happened. Pepper, paint spray and a barrage of water bombs—all interspersed with flashes of light and lusty cries of "Hiya, spooky!" and "Gotcha!"—flew in the direction of the west chimney wall. The chief victim was undoubtedly Muldoon, who soon resembled something that had lately been dragged through a puddle. He was rescued by a voice that bawled hoarsely from the attic door.

"All right! What the devil is going on up here in the middle of the blasted night!"

Silence and sanity returned slowly to the attic as Mr. Sweet surveyed the battleground. Streaks of water ran down the chimney breast. Patches of red paint glistened on the floor, and Bonnie's face was as mottled as if she had the measles. Muldoon shook himself happily and sprayed them all with water from his coat. Mr. Sweet sniffed the air in the attic and wrinkled up his nose.

"Daddy," said Bonnie pleasantly, "we were just trying to photograph the spooks."

"Spooks!" The word practically exploded in Mr. Sweet's lips before he got it out. "Don't talk to me about spooks. All right, that is *it*! There will be no horse. I'll spook the lot of you with the back of my hand!"

And he would have too, were it not for the fact that he got some pepper up his nose at that moment. The Sweet kids escaped while their father coped with a sneezing fit.

10...

Dissatisfied Customers

Up in the attic things were not at all what they used to be.

The ghosts of Mercia Porterhouse drifted at ghost pace on unseen currents of slowly moving air. Lady Cordelia McIntyre turned in large, voluminous circles as the outline of her fingers plucked nervously at the string of ivory figurines around her neck. Sir James Walsingham sniffed snuff, but without enthusiasm, and Bobbie gazed at her bundle of brushes as if these familiar objects had unaccountably become a mystery to her. Perhaps she was listening to the drone of a fire burning steadily in the west chimney.

James had drifted into a vertical, though upside-down, position. His feet were in the air, and his wig almost touched the floorboards.

"I do wish you would make an effort to stay upright, James," said Cordelia.

"What does it matter whether I'm upside down or the right way up?" James responded testily.

"I happen to think it matters. I know that we are mere shadows of our former selves, but I do believe that at least we should try to preserve the outward appearance of normality. You allow yourself to drift all over the place and it is most off-putting."

They were very much on edge. Trapped as they were in Real Time—like all ghosts—the best they could hope for was to pass their days quietly in some favored place, bothering no one and not being bothered in return. In a quiet period of Unwakeful Serenity, five or ten years whizzed by. It wasn't a hard life, being a ghost—at least it hadn't been until now. Now James's carboy was under a bush, Bobbie's chimney felt like an oven and even Rajah's foot had been turned into a coal scuttle.

To make matters worse, all their efforts at haunting had met with dismal failure. Only last evening they had materialized from a grandfather clock—all three of them at once—and the Sweet children had howled with delight as if they were watching a jolly good comedy show at the local theater. Even the dog had jumped right through James as if he were a hoop!

"Oh, for an hour or two of solid flesh!" sighed James, then he turned himself the right way up in order to listen. Outside, doors were slamming.

He joined Cordelia and Bobbie at the tiny attic window. Two cars had pulled up at the front door. People were getting out. A third car appeared from the tunnel of cedar branches, and it too was full of people.

"What the devil do they all want? Eh?" said James crossly.

"Perhaps the family is entertaining."

"Before *lunch*?"

"Either that, James, or these are the first of the paying customers, and they are here to see you, and Bobbie, and me."

The look on James's face, in normal circumstances, would have made Cordelia smile.

She was absolutely right. These were the paying customers, and Hungryhouse Lane had opened for business. At approximately eleven thirty, nine children appeared at the front door, where a freshly painted sign made them agog with excitement:

SPOOK HOUSE: ENTER AT YOUR OWN RISK.

Three sets of parents accompanied the children, and poor Mrs. Sweet, who had *not* been informed that anyone was coming, was obliged to smile at her visitors as if people dropped in on her every day of the week. Privately, however, she was a bundle of nerves.

"They'll expect to be fed. They're probably starving," she cried in the kitchen as if they were five thousand. "Why didn't you tell me they were *coming*, Zoe? Fetch another loaf from the freezer. Stupid children, you invite the whole world and the last one to know about it is me!"

"They're only some of our school friends, Mom," said Zoe.

"And they weren't supposed to bring their moms and dads," added Charlie.

"Rubbish! We live in the country now. How else would they get here, do you think they can *fly*?" Ferociously she attacked a lump of ham. "And what nonsense have you been telling these children? They say they're here to see the spooks. Well, they'll just have to make do with sandwiches!"

With this dire threat she swooped on a tray and disappeared with it.

Lunch was a boring affair. When Mrs. Sweet said sandwiches, she meant sandwiches, and there wasn't so much as a dry cookie to dunk in one's tea. As soon as the children managed to escape, Zoe formed them into a line, and Bonnie took their money as they entered the great parlor. Each of the Sweet kids had contacted three of their school friends. Someone's big brother had come along too, so the takings amounted to the handsome total of three whole pounds. The extra body was a big, aggressive twelve-year-old whose name was Davy.

"If we don't see spooks," he warned, "I want my money back."

"Fat chance," said Zoe Sweet. "Let's go."

The guided tour for the paying customers began with the west chimney, where Zoe described Bobbie as a sooty sort of ghost who wailed in the night. They gathered around the coal scuttle to hear how it was really an elephant's foot, and how it was haunted by a lady in a gorgeous white dress. "A dress like foam," said Zoe. "She admired my roller skates." Finally they mounted the narrow stairs to the attic.

"When the spooks appear," warned Zoe, "we don't want any crybabies. Okay, who's first?"

This was a thrilling moment for the paying customers, but there were no volunteers to go first. Some of them with nervous habits blinked and twitched and swallowed hard. So Charlie went into the attic first, and then there was such a scramble to be second that a pile of wriggling bodies jammed the door.

It was a large, high attic, and the enthralled visitors had all the room they needed to turn and stare at the curious mementos all around them. But soon eyes that had been wide with wonder became cloudy with disappointment, and then with suspicion, for it was quite obvious that there were no spooks.

"I guess you picked a bad day," Bonnie said sympathetically to her little friend Maxine and her brother John.

"Can't you *call* them or something?"

"Don't be silly," Zoe told her friend Vanessa. "I

mean, it's not as if they're dogs or parrots—you can't just whistle them up."

"Well, where are they?"

"How long do we have to wait?"

"Huh! Some spooks!"

Davy scowled ominously. "I came to see ghosts and there are no ghosts. All right, I want my money back."

"Tough," said Zoe.

"What do you mean—tough?"

"Just because you didn't see them doesn't mean there aren't any. That's the risk you take."

"And don't forget what it said on the door," Charlie pointed out. "It said, 'Enter at your own risk.' "

"And our mommy gave you tea and sandwiches," added Bonnie for good measure.

Most of the paying customers were dumbfounded by this turn of events—but not Davy. "You're a bunch of crooks!" he declared, whereupon Zoe let him know with a push in the chest that he should be more careful with his language.

Now Davy pushed Zoe and sent her crashing to the wall. At this point Charlie Sweet stepped forward and said, "Don't you push my sister, or I'll smash your face in."

It was hard to tell who was more surprised—Davy or Zoe, who knew that Charlie had often pushed her himself, and many times harder than Davy had just

done. This was the first time he had ever stuck up for her. She was very pleased.

Perhaps it would be too much to say that war now broke out in the attic. Certainly there was some wrestling on the floor as the Sweet kids and some of their dissatisfied customers did their best to sit on one another. But most of the children stood by and watched, rather like Muldoon—who pranced about the fringes of the fray, adding his voice to the howls of the spectators and the thumps of the struggling bodies on the floor.

Although there was very little damage (some hair pulling, a little arm twisting, but no biting), the din was horrible! Parents rushed upstairs, took one look at their disheveled children and began to say things like, "Really, we must be going," and, "Thank you so much for lunch, yes of course we'll call again," and, "Come along children—*quickly,* please."

The first paying visit to Spook House was over.

Several minutes later, when the noise of battle had died away and the dust had had time to settle in the attic, a shadowy Presence descended from the old chandelier and sat on the edge of the water tank. Lady Cordelia materialized from the vicinity of the doll's house, and Bobbie, preceded by her brushes, made an entrance through the west chimney wall.

Only James knew what to make of what they had

just seen. "Barbarians!" he cried. "That's what they are, you know—we're up against barbarians!"

"There is only one person who can help us," Cordelia said pensively. "We must visit our friend Amy and tell her what has been happening."

"What can *she* do?" James asked huffily.

"Perhaps nothing at all, James. But do you have a *better* idea? . . ."

11...

Oggi Agga Gooth, Tiger Woman

Amy Steadings turned her Closed sign to face the street, pulled down the blinds, slotted the top and bottom bolts of the door, and then returned to the rear of the shop. It was the end of another day of doing business. Amy shooed the cat off her chair, took up her knitting and finished a ball of wool.

"There now," she said aloud, quietly satisfied. The blanket for Unicef was coming along nicely. Amy liked to think of little children in faraway countries snuggling down into her wool: Somehow it made her feel warm too.

The kettle sang on the stove. Over a cup of tea she read again the letter from the estate agent.

> *Dear Ms. Steadings,*
>   *My clients have authorized me to raise their offer on the above property by a further £1,500.*

They feel it is a fair price for your premises in their present state of repair, and I hope you will consider their offer seriously. . . .

And so on. Well, maybe I *should* sell, thought Amy. Young business people with a lot of go in them would pull down a wall here and there and turn her place into an antique shop or an "olde worlde tea parlour," and why not? It wasn't as if people bought tobacco the way they used to do when her father was alive—no doubt they would find her a modern little house with central heating and a proper working kitchen. It might be nice.

"But it might not be nice at all," Amy reminded herself. And as if to answer her, someone behind her gave a little cough.

Amy spun around, heart beating—but it was only James. "What a lovely surprise!" she cried. "I'm so pleased to see you, James. How are you?"

"Awful," said James.

Amy clapped her hands with delight to see that Cordelia and skinny little Bobbie had come too.

"It must be six or seven years since I've seen you. How I wish I could make you all a lovely cup of Darjeeling tea. You must tell me all your news."

The news, of course, was thoroughly bad from start to finish. It took Cordelia but a few minutes to tell how Zoe, Bonnie and Charlie Sweet were turning the house in Hungryhouse Lane upside down and making life a misery.

"You poor dears!" cried Amy.

"And I'm afraid I may have mentioned the will to them," said Cordelia. "Do you think it will matter?"

"Oh, I shouldn't think so. I've given up all hope of finding dear Mercia's will after all this time. I wish there was something I could do to help you."

James, who had not spoken for some time, suddenly roused himself. "I've been thinking. Couldn't you go to Hungryhouse Lane and steal my carboy? You could grab Cordelia's elephant's foot too, and we could live here with you."

"Shame on you, James!" exclaimed Cordelia. "What about poor Bobbie? Do you expect Amy to steal the west chimney, too? That is a sordid idea if ever I heard one."

James, who loathed criticism, allowed himself to tilt sideways until he reached an angle of forty-five degrees.

"Really," said Amy, "I am most disappointed in those children, I really am. And you say that you tried to frighten them?"

"It didn't work, though. In fact they seemed to enjoy it."

"Hmm," Amy mused thoughtfully. "What would happen, though, if they saw a really frightening ghost? I don't mean to offend you dear people, but you're not exactly the sort to make those children quake in their boots. No. . . . What we need for them is a ghost who is just as nasty as they are—one who enjoys scaring people half to death."

"Is there such a thing?" Cordelia asked doubtfully.

"There certainly is, my dear! Mercia used to know one exactly like that in Scotland."

"Scotland! The ends of the earth!" cried James.

"Not nowadays, James. We could be there and back in a day in my little hatchback."

"*We?* You mean all of us?"

"Of course I do. I'm not going all that way on my own." Amy suddenly clapped her hands once and looked happy. "Oh, this is such a good idea. It will be a lovely adventure for all of us, wait and see!"

To the many truckers who passed the little blue hatchback in the inside lane, it must have seemed that here was yet another crazy old lady talking to herself on the northbound freeway. But they were wrong. Amy Steadings was not alone. She had three almost invisible companions to talk to.

"Mercia read about her in some sort of ancient book," Amy explained just south of Manchester, "and went to visit her one summer. Apparently she is the oldest ghost in the British Isles. Her name is Oggi Agga Gooth, the Tiger Woman."

Dear me, thought Cordelia. Such a mouthful!

"And," continued Amy, "according to Mercia, she is a remarkable ghost. Full of energy and drive. Full of life!"

74...

"A ghost," James piped up, "cannot be full of life. That's exactly what they're not full of. A ghost is an ex-human being and therefore empty of life."

He was situated somewhere in the vicinity of the front seat. It frequently crossed his mind how the times had certainly changed since he was flesh and blood. In his day you were lucky to get to Scotland in less than three weeks.

"Oh, do be quiet, James. Please go on, Amy. You were describing this Scottish ghost to us."

"She's not really Scottish. Oggi Agga Gooth is prehistoric and lived in the Stone Age, long before anybody thought of calling Scotland Scotland. It seems that they built a castle over the cave where she was killed thousands of years ago by a saber-toothed tiger."

"The Stone Age?" asked Cordelia, tentatively.

"Yes. The human race is a great deal older than they used to think in the eighteenth century. There was a time when people used stone knives and tools and things." How jolly uncouth, thought James, who could not imagine sitting down to dinner with a stone knife and fork.

Traveling through a fine drizzle, they passed through the town of Carlisle and over the border into Scotland. James complained that the slap of the wipers on the windshield was making him dizzy. "It's not far now," said Amy.

They approached the castle down the side of a valley. It had been built on a granite crag and was centrally situated in a loop formed by a meandering river. At the misty edge of the plain a rim of low hills was barely visible. The scene was just as Mercia had described it to Amy. The hatchback suddenly began to go rather fast as she became excited.

"Now," Amy said in the parking lot, "unfortunately I cannot go through walls like you three, so I shall join you inside. Wait for me in the portrait gallery. Dear me, I'm all of a fluster. Off you go."

Using special ghost techniques to counterbalance the effects of a playful breeze, Cordelia, James and Bobbie penetrated the outer defenses of the castle. The portrait gallery was a high, gloomy building, perfectly suited to the rows of gloomy gentlemen hanging there in gilded frames. There wasn't a smile among them. Cordelia wondered whether they had ever had a moment's happiness.

"Of course, this reminds me," James said uppishly, "of Sir Alan Gilzean's place in the country. I had lunch there with Walpole, you know."

"Such a pity, James," said Cordelia, "that you ended up in a glass bottle."

Amy arrived in a breathless rush, complaining that she'd had such a keen young fellow for a guide. "I had quite a job to slip away. Come along, we have to go down to the dungeons."

So down they went, into those hollow, scooped-out caverns where Amy's heels seemed to echo on and on for ages each time she paused for breath.

"Bless us!" she puffed. "That Mercia must have had the constitution of an ox. I think one more flight of these steps and that will have to do."

By now they had arrived in the foundations of the castle, and the steps had evidently been hewn from the very rock.

"Excuse me," said Amy, rather timidly, "but is there anyone here? We are looking for a ghost called Oggi Agga Gooth. Can you help us, please?"

"What a silly name. What a beastly place," muttered James.

One moment they were looking at a rough, bare wall stained with patches of green moss, and the next they were looking at an extraordinary shape that seemed to pour out through cracks in the stones. The Tiger Woman was dressed in . . . well, in hardly anything at all, really. James was thoroughly scandalized. A bearskin covered some of her bare skin, and the head of the bear was plainly visible. Her hair fell to her waist with neither curl nor wave—it was as straight as a horse's tail. And the coils of a vicious whip caressed her knobby feet.

"State your business," said this apparition. The eyes were dark holes in a fiercely shimmering head.

Amy began to stammer. Oggi Agga Gooth was even more breathtaking than Mercia had painted her.

"Well, you see . . . oh dear. My friends here, these . . . eh . . . ghosts, like yourself . . . Well, frankly they are having some difficulties at the moment."

"Difficulties, eh?" The whip gave a single flick, and a snakelike effect ran all the way to the tip. What can she use a thing like that *for*? thought Cordelia.

Amy explained the situation as best she could, alluding to the rather gentle nature of her three friends. "All we want to do," she finished, "is to get rid of those terrible children and get back to the way we were."

Oggi Agga Gooth wiped her nose with a piece of bearskin. "Try haunting them."

"We did show ourselves," Cordelia ventured to say, "and we did wail in the night, but it didn't work. In fact, one might say that it made matters ten times worse. They now intend to exhibit us as . . . as specimens."

"Och, woman, wailing is not enough," said Oggi Agga Gooth. "Did you try laughing at them by any chance?"

"Laughing at them?"

"Aye! Make it loud and mad and wild, like this." And she proceeded to demonstrate. Back went the head, which seemed to become a mass of swirling hair and gappy teeth. The horrible, cackling chuckle had an uncanny effect on Amy, who felt it in the very gums under her false teeth.

"That's the way to do it. There's something about laughing that they can't stand. I can easily stampede a whole castleful of tourists with a laugh like that. Have you tried carrying your head?"

Cordelia fingered her necklace anxiously. She felt so innocent and silly. "What exactly do you mean?"

Oggi Agga Gooth removed her head and stuck it under her arm. The hair, instead of reaching to her waist, now trailed the ground.

"This never fails," said the head under the armpit.

"By the Lord Harry!" said James.

"Then I let them see Sabba!" cried the Tiger Woman, flexing her whip. "Here, my pet. To me, to me. Psst!"

Amy Steadings, who was really quite used to ghosts and to many of their ways, nevertheless almost jumped out of her skin. Lady Cordelia McIntyre, who had faced the tigers of Bengal, nevertheless gaped in awesome wonder at the new apparition. The beast snatching at the air with venomous claws was at least as big as a donkey. The lips in the massive, tossing head curled back to reveal a set of gross, impossible fangs. This beast, like something from a childhood dream, crouched there sitting and roaring until it responded, at last, to the voice of its mistress.

"Och, control yourself, you big lump, or I'll have to give you a good hiding!"

Amy was breathless but ecstatic. "Oh yes! Your forceful personality is exactly what we need. Please say that you will help us. I will take you in my hatchback— and bring you back again, of course."

"We should be ever so grateful," said Cordelia.

"Och, why not?" said Oggi Agga Gooth. "Sure it'll be a wee bit of a change for us, won't it, Sabba?"

80...

"You surely don't intend to bring that *beast*?" cried James.

"Oh, do be sensible, James," said Amy. "This is exactly what we have been looking for. Those children have had everything their own way up until now. Now we'll see how they cope with a *proper* haunting!"

12...

A Secret Place

It was half past nine in the morning.

Charlie Sweet sat on the sunny back step of the house in Hungryhouse Lane. Stretched out at his feet on a warm patch of ground was Muldoon Moonbug Nelson Sweet, who seemed at that moment like the most contented creature on earth. Now and then some part of him twitched, as if a fly had tickled an ear, or a dream his imagination.

His young master was not so thoroughly at peace with the world. Charlie's sisters had ganged up on him again—this time because he had taken pictures of them while they were shampooing their hair. They did not want the whole world to see them with their hair glued down by oodles of white foam. Indeed, they would have taken the film out of his camera there and then had it not also contained the photos of the ghosts in the attic. Instead they decided to pretend that Charlie Sweet did not exist and went into the village without him. They tried to get Muldoon on their side as well, but the dog was too loyal or too idle to budge.

Birds twittered in the wood. From the kitchen came the faint click of dice on board. A rumble in Charlie's tummy reminded him of how hungry he was, so he got up and went into the kitchen.

"Double fours!"

"Lucky."

"You got double sixes. Luck evens out, you know."

"I hate to butt in," said Charlie, "but I haven't had any breakfast."

"Eat some cornflakes," said Mr. Sweet.

"I don't want cornflakes."

"Then microwave something, Charlie dear," said Mrs. Sweet.

"I guess I could microwave my frog spawn," Charlie mumbled somewhat bitterly, "if I could find them."

"Fine, dear." The dice rolled, *clickety-click*. "And *again*, double fours!"

"Lucky, lucky duck," said Mr. Sweet.

Charlie ate some cornflakes. Muldoon waited with bated breath for the tidbit that never came. When Charlie got up, he went straight to Bonnie's room.

He was thinking about those taddies. There was a very good chance that he would never see those frog spawn again, and his sister was the reason why. Okay, if she wanted to play rough . . .

Lulubelle Sweet was lying nicely tucked up in bed, smiling up at Charlie with her red thread smile. Stupid doll. You wouldn't be smiling, thought Charlie, if you knew where you were going.

Two minutes later Charlie stood under the yawning black hole that was the west chimney. Up he went, step by step, with the aid of an aluminum ladder, watched all the way by a rather nervous-looking Muldoon. Charlie was about to set Lulubelle on a ledge when he noticed something rather odd. There were stone steps in the chimney—three of them. And they led directly to a small door.

Funny. Why should there be a door in a chimney? Such an odd, arch-shaped little thing it was, with a knob about the size of his fist. Along the bottom ran the thinnest possible chink of light, as if someone was at work in there. . . . Aware of his quickening heartbeats, Charlie eased it open.

He found himself looking into a small room, lit from above by a domed window. The rough stone walls had been neither painted nor papered, and so the place had the appearance of a cave. The two pieces of furniture were an old-fashioned writing desk and a high chair with its back to him.

Suppose, thought Charlie, just suppose there was someone sitting in it—dead! It was a ridiculous idea,

a spurt of his imagination, but it didn't quite leave him until he took a pace or two into the room and found that it was occupied only by a book. The words on the cover said *Five Year Diary* in gold lettering.

Charlie opened it at random. The writing was very good—much better than his teacher could manage on the school chalkboard.

> *Well, my dear friends have not been with me for some years. It makes me happy to think that they are so peaceful. I have heard of another Presence who lives down a well on Blacksford Manor, but I don't know what to do. If I ask the owner to sell me his well, he'll think me quite mad, I'm sure. Besides, how would I get it here. . . .*

At first Charlie didn't know what to make of the book. Then he came across a name he recognized:

> *Amy rode out this evening on that old black bicycle she's got. The thing is an antique! And her news is that she's bought a car and is learning to drive! At your age, I said, whereupon she reminded me that she is twenty years younger than I, and beat me at two games of backgammon for being so presumptuous. Oh yes, and the sparrows have hatched in the barn.*

It's that old bird's diary, thought Charlie—the one who used to live here. "Maybe she's a spook herself by now," he said aloud, and turned to the beginning of the book.

Guess what—I saw James for the first time in ages this evening. We listened to some Mozart. James says that Mozart was a skinny little chap—claims he saw him at a concert in Vienna. Dear old James, he does give himself grand airs. I think he was offended when I suggested that perhaps he was telling me a bit of a fib. Turned himself upside down for ages!

Charlie threw down the diary and turned his attention to the rest of the room. A layer of dust had settled on the top of the desk like a fine fur. It covered the pipe rack and obscured the handwritten title on the cover of an old file. Blowing off the dust, Charlie read, *The Ghosts of Great Britain: An Account of Their Whereabouts* BY MERCIA PORTERHOUSE. Glancing through it, Charlie saw that there were spooks everywhere from Cornwall to the tip of Scotland, and that hardly anybody knew they were there because they passed the time doing as little as possible. Just like that dozy tortoise I used to have, thought Charlie, stooping to pick up the long document with the red ribbon around it that had just fallen out of the file. It said THE LAST WILL AND TESTAMENT OF MERCIA PORTERHOUSE.

This was her private place, thought Charlie, her secret room, and nobody knew about it—not a soul. If she'd died here, she would still be here, sitting in that chair, waiting to be discovered along with her books and her will. And now it was *his* secret room, Charlie

Sweet's personal hiding place—nobody in the whole world could find him here. What a super idea!

Of course, the place had to be photographed. In a hurry now he threw the will aside and made his way down the ladder as quickly as he could without breaking a leg. He was back in two minutes with his camera. Working quickly, in case his sisters came back, he took four snapshots of the room before the film refused to wind any further. The roll was finished. He would have to take it into the village to get it developed.

Charlie waved good-bye to Lulubelle and left the secret room.

13...

A Proper Haunting

onnie Sweet saw it first.

She had just changed into her nice clean nightie with the pink flowers around the hem when the spook appeared at her bedside table. It was black and white and beckoned with one eerie finger as it said in a hoarse and horrible voice, "Come here, my little girl. I want you."

Bonnie stiffened like an icicle, for there was something about this thing that wasn't quite like the other spooks. Maybe it was that whip. . . . And she wasn't wearing any proper clothes, either.

"I want you to go away," said Bonnie.

The ghost's mouth produced a cackle of a laugh. Mesmerized, Bonnie watched that tongue move inside the hollow head. "Not without you, my little pigeon. You must come too."

"Come where?" Bonnie's voice was a whimper.

"*Never mind!* Just do what you're told, my little Bonnie girl, and I'll treat you nice!"

This spook knows my *name*, thought Bonnie. It began to move forward slowly, still beckoning, and Bonnie, seeing right through the advancing ghost, suddenly felt a massive scream inside her trying to get out, for she saw her pillow was bare and Lulubelle was gone. The spook had put a spell on her and whisked her away to the Kingdom of the Spooks!

Bonnie closed her eyes, the shriek came out and she took off in terror.

Zoe too was getting ready for bed in a happy mood. She was thinking how readily her friend Vanessa and the others had agreed to pay thirty pence to see the spooks. We should have charged fifty pence, Zoe thought gleefully. Of course, it was a pity that the ghosts hadn't actually appeared, but that was probably a small problem and could be put right with a little thought. Maybe the television people would come and make a film about the ghosts of Hungryhouse Lane, and the Sweet children would be famous all over the world. . . . Such were her thoughts when the bedroom door burst open and Bonnie burst in like a tornado.

"Zoe! Oh, Zoe, there's another spook, a really wicked one, she's got Lulubelle and she's after me, too."

"Don't be so silly, Bonnie."

"I'm not being silly. She's taken Lulubelle away to

the Kingdom of the Spooks and she said my actual *name*."

Zoe took Bonnie's trembling little shoulders in her hands and spoke to her firmly. "It can't take anybody anywhere. It's only a spook, and there's not a thing it can do to you. Come on, you can sleep in my bed tonight."

But Zoe did not see, as she approached the four-poster bed, how the closed bed curtains suddenly rippled all the way around. When she threw back the curtains, her heart jumped into her throat with a truly terrifying jolt and seemed to stop there—for a headless vapor stood but an arm's length from her nose.

The worst thing was, though, that the spook *did* have a head, but not in the proper place. The spook's head was under its arm, from where it suddenly breathed a single word: "Zoe-eeeee."

Now the head laughed so madly that it came loose and drifted to the bed, and from the bed to the floor, where it kept right on going and turning, a weightless tangle of hair rolling toward Zoe's toes—and talking as it came! "It's you I want, Zoe, ma wee pet." Then the rest of the spook stepped smartly off the bed and followed its head.

For a few agonizing seconds Zoe's poor legs failed to do what she was telling them to. Then at last she bolted.

Charlie Sweet was throwing darts when the big cat came through the wall. It took time to measure him with a cool, long stare, then up it rose on powerful hind legs—a snarling, towering Presence that seemed to fill the room. The massive head passed through the light shade, allowing Charlie a fine view of the beast's incredible fangs and the angry foam at the corners of its gaping jaws. Charlie let loose a dart at it, then flung himself sideways against the wall. The panic-stricken Muldoon clawed wildly at the crack under the door, hoping to escape that way. When the crack didn't get any bigger, he simply lay down as if he were dead.

The girls burst in just in time to catch a glimpse of the beast as it faded through the wall, still writhing and spitting to the end. And they continued to stare at the washed-out wallpaper long after it had gone.

"Charlie! What was that *thing*?"

Charlie wiped the sweat from his brow. It felt like cold grease.

"I don't know. Some kind of big cat. Boy, that was a bit scary."

Muldoon, hearing the sound of familiar voices, cheered up immensely. He gave himself a good shake and wandered over to lick Zoe's hand as she described to Charlie the headless spook that had given her and Bonnie such a fright.

"I'm scared," whispered Bonnie almost tearfully. "That ghost knows my name and she's got Lulubelle and she's going to get me and take me away to the Kingdom of the Spooks."

"There's no such place, moonbeam," said Zoe.

"And she hasn't got Lulubelle," said Charlie.

"She *has*. I tucked her up in bed and she isn't there anymore. She's gone."

This wasn't an act—Charlie could see that his sister was genuinely suffering, so for once he decided to be merciful. He even put his arm around her shoulder. "She hasn't got Lulubelle. I hid her because you stole my frog spawn, that's all."

"Oh, Charlie!" There was hero worship in Bonnie's eyes. "I thought that spook had her. Your big bottle's under a bush in the garden, and I'm really really sorry about your horrible frog spawn. Did you bury her?"

"No. She's up in the secret room."

At once Zoe left off tickling Muldoon behind the ears in order to give her full attention to that last remark.

"Secret room? What secret room?"

"The old lady who owned this house had a secret room, and I found it."

"Where is it?"

"You'd never guess. You wouldn't find it in a hundred years, and I'm not telling."

"Be like that, Charlie," said Zoe in the tone of one who refuses to beg. "Anyway, we've got this spook to think about. What are we going to do if it comes back? That's what I'd like to know."

The Sweet kids, who were not cowards (except for Muldoon), began to draw up their battle plans.

14...

The Sweet Kids
Versus the Tiger Woman

Charlie's bed was empty, and so was Bonnie Sweet's. They were all in Zoe's room behind the drawn curtains of the four-poster bed, waiting.

"Do you think she'll come?" whispered Bonnie. "Maybe she won't come."

"She'll come all right," said Zoe.

"I hope she comes," said Charlie.

Muldoon, who lay stretched out along the foot of the bed, gave a worried little grunt and stirred uneasily in his sleep.

None of them had changed for bed—somehow they felt more confident with their daytime clothes on. Zoe's fingers played nervously with the trigger of the hair dryer on her lap. Bonnie too had a hair dryer, though her hair wasn't in the least bit wet. The middle of the bed was occupied by a large vacuum cleaner and its various attachments. The Sweet children weren't exactly comfortable as they sat there, because of the extension cords lying everywhere in coils. But this was a matter of no importance, for they did not intend to go to sleep just yet.

Suddenly Muldoon pricked up his ears and glared at the curtains.

"What do you think?" mouthed Zoe.

"Dunno. Listen," said Charlie.

He opened his camera and got it ready. There hadn't been a drugstore in Tunwold Village, but luckily enough the old lady in the tobacco shop had been able to sell him a roll. She'd also promised to send his finished film to the next big town for developing. The deliverymen were used to that sort of thing in the country, she said. Soon Charlie would know whether it was possible to photograph spooks.

From beyond the curtain came the sound of gruff breathing interspersed with grunts and deep, throaty growls.

"I think it's the monster!"

Bonnie was exactly right. The silence was suddenly split by an uninhibited, unearthly roar. The spook with the detachable head was there too—they heard her cackle and say, "Where are you all, my pigeons? I've come for you!"

Zoe Sweet flung back the curtain of her bed, saw

the Tiger Woman, watched her whip uncoil across the room, heard her cat-beast hiss and snarl, and yelled at the top of her voice, "All right! Switch on and get stuck in!"

The ambush began with the whirr of electrical gadgets starting up. Bonnie, being the smallest, pointed her hair dryer at the spook's legs and blew them clean away. Then she zapped a hole right through its middle.

Zoe aimed her attack directly at the venomous head of the cat-beast and blasted it right out of shape. Gone were the jagged fangs and the slashing paws and the wicked, hollow eyes.

"Woo-ee!" cried the Sweet kids.

"Up your nose!"

"Wacker-doo!"

As pieces of ghost began to float about the room like so much cotton candy, even Muldoon got into the action by pawing at bits of Oggi Agga Gooth as they slid slowly down a curtain. Charlie, meanwhile, had started up the vacuum cleaner, and while his sisters ran about the room blowing, he ran about the room sucking. Bits of saber-toothed tiger disappeared ignominiously up the cleaner brush.

Suddenly it was all over. Nowhere in the room did there remain a trace of spook. The victory of the Sweet kids was total and complete. Bonnie was so happy that she sang two verses of *Ghostbusters*.

"All right, Charlie," Zoe said in a businesslike tone of voice. "I want to see that secret room."

"Now?"

"Why not now?"

Charlie shrugged his shoulders as if now was as good a time as any.

Up the chimney they went—including Muldoon, who howled like a spoiled child until they passed him up from one pair of hands to another as if he were a parcel.

It was strange how they whispered to one another when they got up there. Zoe, at least, seemed to understand that the room was every bit as private and personal as the diary that lay open on the table under the soft glow of a table lamp. "I bet she sat up here smoking her pipe," she said quietly, leafing through the ghost book of Mercia Porterhouse. "There are spooks everywhere, according to this book. Here's one who lives in a lighthouse in Kent. And look, this one from the Isle of Man rides on a tractor!"

"A real tractor?" asked Bonnie as she smoothed Lulubelle's pigtails.

"Don't be stupid. The tractor's a ghost too. Throw over that paper with the ribbon around it, Charlie."

Charlie obliged, and Zoe made short work of untying the ribbon. "You know what? Amy Steadings *does* own this house—it says so in black and white. This is the lost will. And that lady ghost was right. We shouldn't be here."

"Tough," said Charlie. "We *are* here."

"Yes," said Zoe, a little doubtfully. "I suppose you're right."

They left the room as they had found it, except that Bonnie took Lulubelle, of course, and Zoe brought with her the book about ghosts for bedtime reading.

15...

A Ray of Hope

It would be difficult to imagine a more dispirited group of ex-human beings than those who gathered at Amy Steadings's house in Tunwold Village.

Even Amy herself looked rather washed-out after driving Oggi Agga Gooth, Tiger Woman, back to Scotland. That unfortunate ghost had scarcely said a word during the whole journey. It was very likely, thought Amy, that she would never be the same again after being blown into small pieces by those Sweet children. They had thoroughly demoralized one of the oldest ghosts in the business.

And now poor James, Cordelia and Bobbie were entirely at their mercy. The house in Hungryhouse Lane was about to become a tourist attraction.

James was evidently thinking the same thing.

"Well, that's it, then, isn't it? We're finished. It's all over." He spoke with one foot on Amy's mantelpiece and an elbow on the fender. "What price now, Unwakeful Serenity? Good-bye sunshine, hello rain!"

Cordelia told him bluntly to be quiet. "You never seem to understand, James, that some things are better left unsaid."

"Are they, by jove! The fact is that those horrors have beaten us hollow. Speaking personally, I am quite prepared to make the best of a bad job."

"Meaning what, James?"

"Meaning that I shall come here and live in a tobacco jar." He glanced guiltily at Bobbie. "When all is said and done, one must look after oneself, after all."

"And what about Bobbie?" asked Cordelia.

"She can find herself another chimney, can't she? There's one behind me. Good grief, a chimney is a chimney!"

"I'm afraid that won't be possible, James," said Amy. "You see . . . I've decided to sell my house. The business is very tiring, and I've had a very good offer for my property."

"Oh, wonderful!" said James. "Just wonderful!" He laid himself down along the hearth and fed his nose some mighty sniffs of snuff. It was a fine exhibition of pique.

Just then Amy's letter box flapped vigorously as something was stuffed through it. She returned with a packet of photographs that the grocer's deliveryman had just brought back from the drugstore in town.

Amy began to turn the snapshots through her fingers in an idle sort of way. The first two were close-ups of frog spawn. Next appeared some views of Mercia's house and a long shot of Jackson's scarecrow. The boy seemed quite a competent photographer, though Amy wondered why on earth there should be five or six pictures of the bare walls in the attic. After a shot of the girls with soapy heads, Amy found herself looking at a picture of a doll sitting in a chair beside a book, for all the world as if the doll were reading it.

Amy's heart gave a slight flutter as she peered more closely at the letters on the cover of the book: *The Ghosts of Great Britain*, it said.

Oh, mercy on us! she thought, rising to her feet. "This is it! Her book! The one that was never found."

The very next picture made Amy gasp. There, on a writing desk, was a document with a red band around it.

"Ah dear me! I feel quite dizzy. Cordelia, come here. James, Bobbie! I really think that this must be Mercia's will—what do you think?"

The ghosts of Mercia Porterhouse had not lived long enough to make a will, but they gathered around the photograph in some excitement.

"Where is that place?" said Cordelia. "I don't recognize it, do you, James?"

He didn't. And Amy refused to believe it. "You *must*

104...

know it. Surely you must have passed through all those walls a hundred times!"

"I suppose it could be one of the outbuildings," Cordelia said doubtfully, then broke off to observe the antics of Bobbie, who had suddenly begun to nod as vigorously as a ghost can nod and was now pointing at the chimney with her brushes.

"Silly little fool," muttered James. "What has got into her?"

But Cordelia understood. "Wait. Bobbie—has this room got something to do with the chimney?" There were more nods, accompanied by brush thrusts. "It's *in* the chimney. She knows it, she's been there!"

"Of course!" cried Amy. "Mercia must have had it built when the chimney was added to the house. That's why it was never found. Oh, she was a deep one, she loved things like that! If we can get that will, the Sweets will have to leave. Don't you see? Everything will be just the way Mercia meant it to be!"

It was exactly the kind of pick-me-up they needed. Cordelia, propelled by a mysterious ghostly locomotion, rose a full foot into the air in excitement.

"Wouldn't it be wonderful!" she said.

"Oh yes, it would be wonderful," said James, who could never look on the bright side of things, "except that the little horrors have probably burned it by now!"

It really was fascinating!

Zoe, tucked up in her four-poster bed, came to the

end of the last chapter of the book about British ghosts.

"Unwakeful Serenity," she read, "is a condition necessary to the well-being of most ghosts. Prolonged Presence in the Real World is painful for them, because they remember, you see, they remember everything, unlike you or me and the great majority of people, who are offered the gift of forgetfulness."

And so the book ended. Zoe closed it thoughtfully, wondering for a moment what it would be like to be alive as a ghostly version of herself a hundred years, or two hundred years, from now—say, like that little sweep—with Mommy and Daddy dead, and Charlie too, and Bonnie . . . and yet remembering everything and not being able to forget . . .

"Oooo," she said with a shiver, and she remembered the coal in the elephant's foot and the carboy still outside in the garden. "I almost feel sorry for our poor old spookies!" Then she put out the light and fell asleep.

But it seemed no time at all before she was awake and sitting up in bed again. There had been a noise— she was sure of it!—in the great parlor. Zoe threw back the covers to investigate.

The door was ajar, and she could see through the crack to the chimney. There was Bobbie, standing in the hearth, where a low fire burned. But she was *real*, and not a ghost at all!

"There you are," said Bobbie. "We'd better get started before 'e comes."

"What do you mean?" said Zoe.

Bobbie squinted up at her from a sooty face. "You don't 'alf talk funny sometimes. Let's go." And so saying, she skipped nimbly up the chimney in such a way as to avoid the hot bricks.

A man dressed in funny clothes, looking like somebody out of *Oliver Twist,* came into the room. "What's keeping you, then?" he barked. "Up you go!"

Zoe glanced down at her bare, black feet and her baggy trousers.

He meant her!

Yes, of course, she saw that this was expected of her. She was dressed for the job; she had to go. Avoiding the hottest part of the fire, as Bobbie had done, she stepped into the chimney and began to climb into the suffocating dark.

Zoe woke up then, thrashing with her feet at the clinging tangle of blankets around her head and throat. With one hand she clawed wildly for the lamp until ages passed, and at last a flood of light banished the darkness, the images and the dream. . . .

16...

A Change of Heart

Saturday morning's breakfast was a weird affair in Hungryhouse Lane. The Sweet kids weren't like themselves at all.

Zoe came into the kitchen with red rims around her eyes, and Bonnie immediately guessed the reason why.

"You've been crying!" she exclaimed. "Charlie— Zoe's been crying."

It was an awesome sight. She, Bonnie, could turn on the waterworks at the drop of a hat, but Zoe never cried—she was much too tough and grown-up for tears. And Bonnie didn't like it when people cried who weren't supposed to cry. It made the world more difficult to understand.

"Zoe, what's wrong? Please don't cry."

"I am not crying."

Not *now*, she wasn't. But she had been. And why was she buttering toast with such a look of misery on her face?

"Would you like to call our horse Jiffy?" Bonnie said, hoping to see a smile. "Would you? We can call our horse Jiffy if you like. I won't mind."

It was a powerful concession, but it didn't work.

"I know what's wrong with her," said Charlie. "She's been reading that book about the spooks."

"What did it say?"

"I don't want to talk about it," said Zoe.

"I want you to *tell* me," demanded Bonnie, furiously.

"No."

This was not a word Bonnie liked to hear, and it often caused a temper tantrum, but not on this occasion. She said, "Please, Zoe, I'd like to know."

"You'll not like it."

"Tell me anyway."

"All right. Once upon a time there was a little baby, and she was born in a haystack in 1831."

"In a *haystack*?"

"Are you going to listen, Bonnie, or not listen?" There was a nod in favor of listening. "All right. Her mommy didn't want her, so she gave the little baby away to strangers, and they gave her to somebody else, so she had about four mommies and daddies by the time she was five."

"Six!" Charlie butted in. He'd read the story too.

"Well, then they cut off her hair and pretended she was a boy instead of a girl, and you know what they did? They made her climb up chimneys and clean them."

"Like a steeplejack person?"

"No, not a bit like a steeplejack person. They made her climb up the *insides* of chimneys. They treated her as if she was some kind of human *brush*. She was never clean, she was always coughing, the soot got in her ears and up her nose and sometimes the creeps didn't even put the fire out and all she had to breathe was filthy, sooty smoke. One time the chimney was so narrow she got stuck."

"What did she do?" Bonnie's lower lip was trembling already.

"They had to pull her down the chimney on a rope, and she broke an arm. Then one day there was a fall of soot halfway up the chimney in Manchester where Bobbie was—her whole head was buried in it. Bobbie tried to wriggle her shoulders and get free but the soot blocked up her nose and her mouth too soon. She tried to shout but she couldn't shout because of the soot going down her throat. Probably that's how the chimney girl died. Swallowing soot. There. You asked me to tell you, and I've told you."

Zoe had hardly stopped talking when Mrs. Sweet in the next room heard the most awful howls of anguish coming from the kitchen. She rushed in to find Bonnie bawling her eyes out on her sister's shoulder. The tears ran down Zoe's face in rivers, and Charlie sat beside them with a face like stone.

"What is it? What's wrong? Girls!" She glared at Charlie. "What have you done to your sisters?"

"Me? I didn't do anything."

"Oh, Mommy, promise me you won't ever make me climb up chimneys and clean them," howled Bonnie.

"Put you up chimneys? Glory be, whatever next?" said Mrs. Sweet, taking over the role of nurse. "Nobody is going to put you up chimneys, for goodness' sake. You've been having bad dreams again, haven't you? Well, that's what comes of all this silly talk about ghosts. Hush now, my pet, there's a good girl. . . ."

Their time was nearly over in Hungryhouse Lane.

Zoe and Charlie Sweet understood that this must be so, because they were old enough to read the diary of Mercia Porterhouse and to see that the house had a special purpose.

Charlie wasn't too sure what that purpose was, but Zoe had more imagination.

"Can't you feel it? Oh yes, I can see it all. That old lady loved everything—starlings, spooks, plants, people, furniture, you name it. It's all got to do with Unwakeful Serenity, Charlie, that's what I think. This is a kind of old-folks' home, only for ghosts, not peo-

112...

ple. It wouldn't surprise me if Mercia was a ghost herself and led you to her secret room."

"She didn't," said Charlie.

"Well, that's what you think, but maybe she did."

And even little Bonnie, who was too young for such deep thoughts, felt that their time was nearly over in Hungryhouse Lane—but for a different reason. She couldn't bear to go into the great parlor, where the west chimney was, in case she had bad thoughts about that sweep who couldn't speak a word.

Mr. and Mrs. Sweet, therefore, were the last to know that they must move. On Monday morning there came a knock at the front door.

"Be a dear and see to the door," said Mrs. Sweet to her husband.

They were scrubbing the bottoms of some old pots. Geoffrey set down his steel wool and saw to the door.

"It's the police," he called.

"The *police*?"

"Yes, dear—the police."

It was one policeman, to be exact, and he loomed large between an elderly woman dressed in dark clothes and a younger woman dressed in light-gray clothes.

"Good afternoon, ma'am. Sir."

Mr. and Mrs. Sweet said "Good afternoon" rather like twin parrots.

"I have reason to believe," said the policeman, talking very like a policeman, "that there may have been an injustice done to this here lady," and he indicated Amy Steadings. "Perhaps you would allow me to investigate up your chimney, sir."

"Up my chimney?"

"Up your chimney, sir. Very much so. We are seeking a missing will."

"Will? Will who?"

"Oh, don't let's dither, Geoffrey. Let the people come in," said Mrs. Sweet. She grabbed Muldoon, who threatened (briefly) to eat the police officer.

Five adults and four Sweet children trooped into the great parlor. The policeman coughed in an embarrassed sort of way, then disappeared up the chimney. Charlie took a photo of his vanishing legs.

The silence while they waited for him to come down again was strained and polite. Mrs. Sweet switched on a silly smile like Lulubelle's each time she caught someone's eye, and all the while she was thinking, There's a policeman up my chimney!

The elderly lady began to fish in her basket for a small package. "There you are, Charlie. Those are your photographs. I do hope you are pleased with them."

"Thanks," said Charlie. "He's wasting his time up there."

"Why is that?" snapped the lady in gray.

"Because it's over here," said Zoe.

She produced a large brown envelope from a drawer and placed it in the hands of the person to whom it was addressed:

114...

Miss Amy Steadings
The Tobacco Shop
Tunwold Village

"Oh dear. No, I don't think I can," said Amy breathlessly; so the lady in gray took it upon herself to draw out the long envelope with the ribbon wrapped around it.

"Incredible! You were right all along, Miss Steadings. This does confirm that you alone are the legal owner of this property."

"Oh. Well! Dear me." Amy's eyes misted over with joy as her lawyer turned now to Mr. and Mrs. Sweet with a very official expression on her face.

"I'm afraid this renders your lease null and void. With due respect and on behalf of my client, I must ask you to vacate these premises in Hungryhouse Lane as soon as possible."

"You mean . . ." Mrs. Sweet's eyes flashed with dismay. ". . . For heaven's sake, Geoffrey. Do you realize that we are *squatters!*"

Let us fast forward our story by nine days and press the pause button at ten forty-five in the morning.

The Sweet family Mercedes leaves the house in Hungryhouse Lane for the last time. Mr. Sweet is slightly worried that he won't make it to a gas station before the car runs out of juice.

Mrs. Sweet is hoping that the carpet fitters and the

painters and the phone people have been into her new house in the city. And if they haven't, why *not*! Her blood pressure rises slightly.

Zoe glances back at the house. With its two watchful eyes and rippling roof now touched by mellow sunshine and set within a frame of cedar branches, she can't help thinking how it would make a terrific jigsaw puzzle. Is that a Presence at one of the upper windows? Probably not.

Bonnie is thinking about the word "jodhpurs," and how it has that funny *h* in the middle. Will there ever be jodhpurs for them? Will there ever be a *horse*?

Charlie wonders why spooks don't come out in photographs. Probably something to do with the film.

Muldoon suddenly scratches violently under his collar, where he is having a running battle with a flea.

In the west chimney Bobbie has already retreated into a state of Unwakeful Serenity.

The outline of Lady Cordelia McIntyre billows softly in the draft from the open skylight as she watches the departure of the Sweet family. What really changed their minds? she wonders. . . .

James is beside her, posted at an annoying angle of forty-five degrees. "And when Amy Steadings dies?" he says. "What happens to us then? Eh?"

In Tunwold Village, Amy Steadings is reading the final entry in the diary of Mercia Porterhouse:

...117

When we are grown up
and have pots of money,
we are going to come
back and buy this house,
spooks and all!

Signed,

Zoe Sweet
Charlie Sweet +
Bonnie Sweet

APPLE®PAPERBACKS

Pick an Apple and Polish Off Some Great Reading!

NEW APPLE TITLES

☐	MT43356-3	**Family Picture** Dean Hughes	$2.75
☐	MT41682-0	**Dear Dad, Love Laurie** Susan Beth Pfeffer	$2.75
☐	MT41529-8	**My Sister, the Creep** Candice F. Ransom	$2.75

BESTSELLING APPLE TITLES

☐	MT42709-1	**Christina's Ghost** Betty Ren Wright	$2.75
☐	MT43461-6	**The Dollhouse Murders** Betty Ren Wright	$2.75
☐	MT42319-3	**The Friendship Pact** Susan Beth Pfeffer	$2.75
☐	MT43444-6	**Ghosts Beneath Our Feet** Betty Ren Wright	$2.75
☐	MT40605-1	**Help! I'm a Prisoner in the Library** Eth Clifford	$2.50
☐	MT42193-X	**Leah's Song** Eth Clifford	$2.50
☐	MT43618-X	**Me and Katie (The Pest)** Ann M. Martin	$2.75
☐	MT42883-7	**Sixth Grade Can Really Kill You** Barthe DeClements	$2.75
☐	MT40409-1	**Sixth Grade Secrets** Louis Sachar	$2.75
☐	MT42882-9	**Sixth Grade Sleepover** Eve Bunting	$2.75
☐	MT41732-0	**Too Many Murphys** Colleen O'Shaughnessy McKenna	$2.75
☐	MT41118-7	**Tough-Luck Karen** Johanna Hurwitz	$2.50
☐	MT42326-6	**Veronica the Show-off** Nancy K. Robinson	$2.75

Available wherever you buy books...or use the coupon below.

Scholastic Inc., P.O. Box 7502, 2932 East McCarty Street, Jefferson City, MO 65102

Please send me the books I have checked above. I am enclosing $_____ (please add $2.00 to cover shipping and handling). Send check or money order — no cash or C.O.D. s please.

Name _____

Address _____

City _____ State/Zip _____

Please allow four to six weeks for delivery. Offer good in the U.S.A. only.
Sorry, mail orders are not available to residents of Canada. Prices subject to change.

APP1089

America's Favorite Series

THE BABY-SITTERS CLUB®

by Ann M. Martin

Collect Them All!

The seven girls at Stoneybrook Middle School get into
all kinds of adventures...with school, boys, and, of course, baby-sitting!